百のうた 千の想い
── 甦る平和百人一首 ──
英訳付

大竹桂子・編
稲田善樹・絵

てらいんく

星野せい　昭和18・2撮影

百のうた　千の想い
──甦る平和百人一首──
英訳付

われら選ぶ人のをさむる新しき
国輝けと一票を投ず

東京　小川登子

We can choose the person to rule our new country. I cast a vote for a brilliant new country.

水(みず)ぬる信濃(しなの)の川(かわ)をよぎる汽車(きしゃ)
はなやぐ子等(こら)の声(こえ)を盛(も)りゆく

新潟　岡田勇五

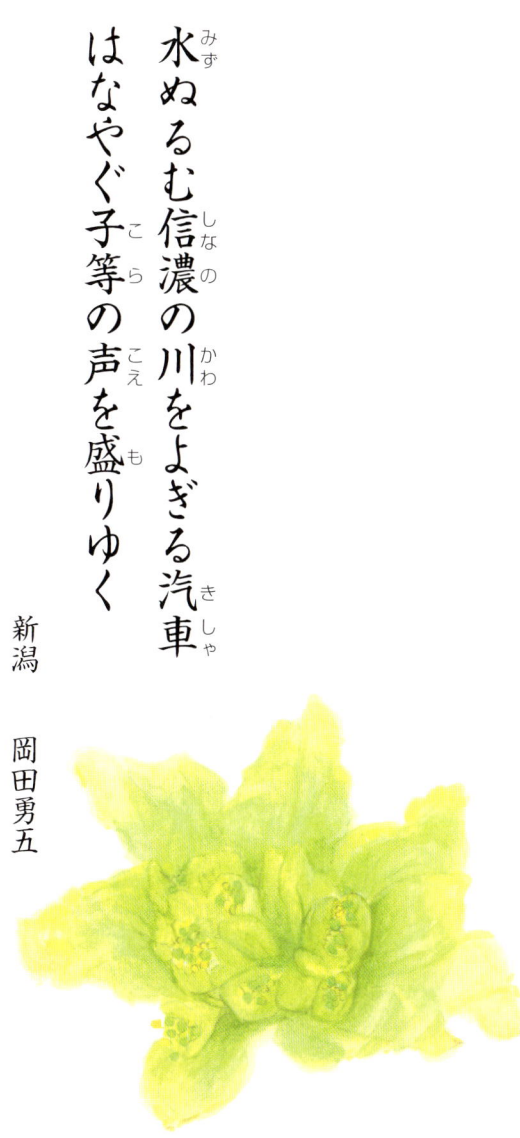

It's getting warmer, spring is coming. I can hear the voices of the children, roused by the steam train crossing the Shinano river

春(はる)は花(はな)秋(あき)はもみじ葉(ば)山河(やまかわ)の
美(う)ましき国(くに)に事(こと)なあらせそ

東京　前田依子

Spring flowers, autumn leaves, I wish for no more hardship in this beautiful country, rich in nature.

うらうらに照る陽を浴みて思ふこと
つつましくしてみちたらひたり

神奈川　鹽崎アキ

In the gentle spring sunlight, I feel so humbly satisfied.

睦み合ふたのしさありて坑内の
荒き業にも耐へてゆくかも

茨城　出久根とき子

We have such a strong and joyous relationship that we can bear such hard work in the mines.

吾(わ)が手(て)もて耕(たがや)し終(お)へし畝間(うねま)より
若芽(わかめ)萌(も)え出(い)づわが心(こころ)にも

群馬　柳谷忠英

As new sprouts are growing from a ridge of my farm. I realize my mind is also blooming.

いく年の苦難の途はひらけたり
わが田となりし土に鍬ふる

東京　戸田武二

After a hard life for many generations, I plough land which is finally my own.

生けるものみな満ち足りて住むといふ
国を思ひぬ春の日かげに

茨城　酒井芳水

Sitting in the sunshine on a pleasant spring day, I imagine a country where all living things live a happy and fulfilled life.

清（すが）しかる朝（あさ）の窓明（まどあ）け今日（きょう）もまた
生命甲斐（いのちかい）ある生活（たつき）祈りぬ

東京　塚野ひろみ

たつき＝生活の手段

Opening the window on a clear, fresh morning, I pray for a way to give my life more meaning.

新(あら)なる国(くに)興(おこ)さむと二千尺(にせんじゃく)
坑底(こうてい)ふかく鶴嘴(つるはし)ふるふ

福岡　安武忠利

My will to build up a new country strengthens as I raise my pickaxe to dig deep into the thousand meter mine.

出坑をまちてゐたりと妻の呼ぶ
声は明るし麦田のなかに

福島　矢内　直

My wife calls out that she has been waiting keenly for me to return from the mine. Her bright voice echoes over the wheat fields.

八千草(やちぐさ)のみだれて匂(にお)ふ春(はる)の野(の)に
みなみの涯(はて)に散(ち)りし恋(こい)恋(こ)ふ

三重　波田かづへ

Standing in the spring field with the smell of thousands of wild flowers. Oh, how I miss my love who I lost in the southern ocean.

外つ国(とつくに)の人も愛(め)づらむ咲(さ)きたりて
日傘(ひがさ)に舞ひ散(ま ち)るさくら吹雪(ふぶき)は

東京　星野せい

Cherry blossoms in full bloom, the petals flutter down upon my parasol like snow. People all around the world must surely appreciate this beauty.

釜(かま)の湯(ゆ)のたぎるしじまに天地(あめつち)の
神(かみ)のこころを思(おも)ひ見(み)るかな

大阪　乾　登代子

A tea ceremony surrounded by silence, the subtle sound of water boiling in the teapot, I can feel God's presence.

地の上に永遠の平和を祈るかな
戦に病みし命生きつつ

千葉　林　房雄

I got sick during the war. However, I could survive and wish for eternal world peace.

春(はる)の野(の)をわが恋(こ)ひくればみなし児(ご)の
くろき片手(かたて)にれんげ匂(にお)へり

埼玉　町田知世子

Oh, how I have longed to see the fields in spring. In an orphan's dirty hand the Renge flower is fragrant.

たたかひは過ぎし夢なり春潮の寄せくる磯に子らと歌ひつ

東京　詩松笙之助

I sing with the children on the sea shore as the spring tide comes in. It seems as if the war was nothing but a dream, since passed.

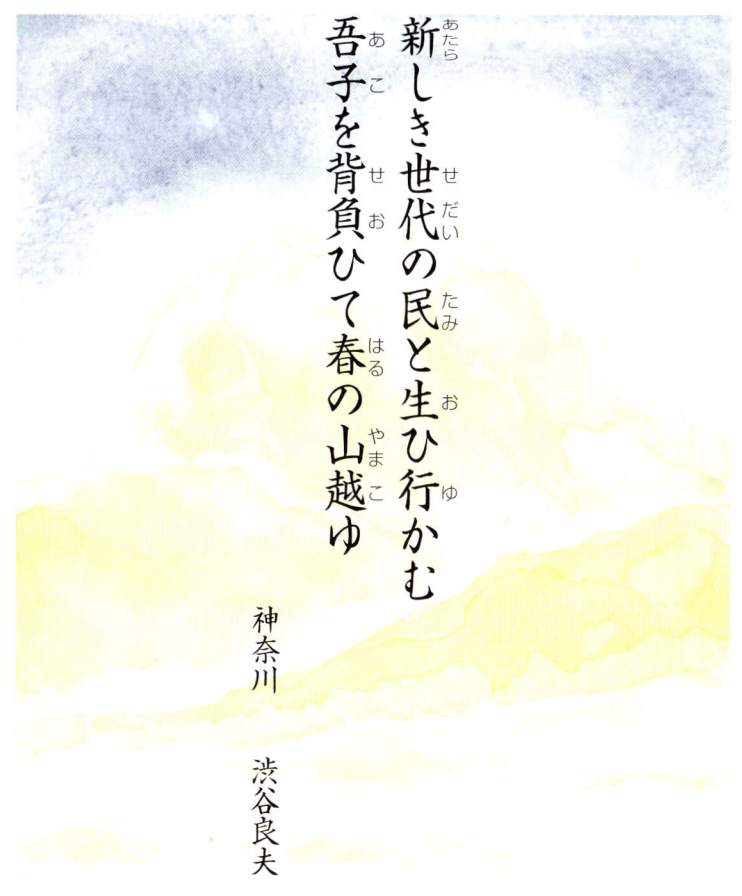

新(あたら)しき世代(せだい)の民(たみ)と生(お)ひ行(ゆ)かむ
吾子(あこ)を背負(せお)ひて春(はる)の山(やま)越(こ)ゆ

神奈川　渋谷良夫

As I carry my child on my back over the mountains in spring, I realize we will live as people in a new world dawning.

かへり来ぬ人のいのちの恋ひしきに
なほ祈らるるいくさなき世を

秋田　高橋園子

I miss my cherished one who didn't make it back. However, I still pray for a world without war.

還り来し父に抱かれ眠る子の
やすけき見れば思ふことなし

兵庫　井上彌生

My child held in the arms of his father who survived the war. I couldn't wish for anything more.

焼跡(やけあと)の瓦(が)れきの中(なか)につはぶきの
芽(め)吹(ぶ)き初(そ)めしか土(つち)割(われ)の見(み)ゆ

静岡　田中龍子

Out of the scorched rubble, a little Tsuwabuki bud is starting to come out. Even it can crack this hardened ground.

街並(まちなみ)は焼(や)けて変(かわ)れど目(め)に触(ふ)るる
すべてなつかし還(かえ)り来(きた)れば

兵庫　片岡忠行

My home town, scorched and reduced to rubble. However, coming back, it all feels familiar and precious.

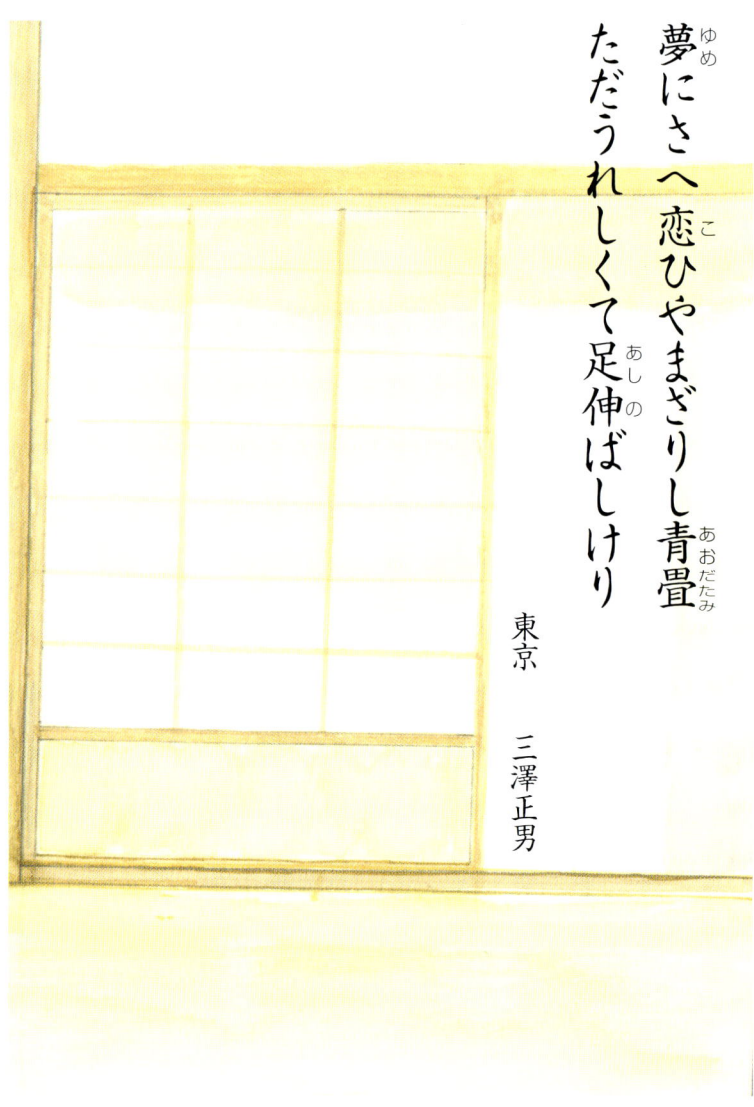

夢(ゆめ)にさへ恋(こ)ひやまざりし青畳(あおだたみ)
ただうれしくて足(あし)伸(の)ばしけり

東京　三澤正男

How I have missed the feeling of a fresh tatami mat. I could see it in my dreams. Simply lying down and stretching my legs on it brings me immense happiness.

大陸の野戦にひとり病みし日を
吾子抱きつつ夫は語りぬ

愛知　瀬尾文子

Holding our son in his arms, my husband tells of his hardest days of the war, alone in the field hospital.

幾千万のいのちやすらぎおほらかに
新憲法は史をかぎるなり

千葉　角田博子

Thousands of lives, cohabitating in peace, our new constitution, a new page in our history.

たたかひに死なざりし命還り来て
桜狩りする春に逢ふかも

和歌山　橋爪　啓

I came back safe and in one piece from the war. I can once again see the cherry blossoms in spring.

いくさなき世となりにけりわがいのち
安けくありて母に仕ふる

東京　鈴木政輝

War is over, now I am finally free to serve and care for my mother.

東(ひむがし)に美(うま)し国(くに)あり矛(ほこ)はすて
海(うみ)に漁(すなど)り土(つち)にいそしむ

東京　伊賀良一

矛＝諸刃(もろは)の剣に長い柄をとりつけた武器
すなどり＝魚を捕らえること

This beautiful country in the East, threw away it's arms and returned to a life of fishing and farming.

われもまた花咲く野辺に手を取りて
子らと遊ばむ春のひとひを

京都　今西米四郎

I too can bask in the fields full of flowers. Holding hands, I play with the children on a spring day.

さきはひはここにこそあれ一つ灯に
親子五人夕餉たのしむ

東京　佐藤暢一

My family of five can get together and enjoy dinner. True happiness is here.

わが明日の命なりけりみどり児に
頬おしあてて憂きは思はず

東京　今井田清子

My beloved child is my tomorrow. We touch cheeks and my worries are gone.

たらちねの母(はは)のひとみを見(み)るたびに
いばらの道(みち)に光(ひかり)さしそふ

東京　橋本　薫

When I look into my mother's eyes, I can see the light at the end of a road of thorns.

萬国に呼びかくるてふ平和塔
われも積ままし清き小石を

岡山　太田資美

For it to be known all around the world as the Peace Pagoda, I would gladly lay a pebble there for world peace.

さむざむと舗道に孤児の佇つ見れば
ふたたびかかるいくさなからしめ

新潟　南雲末子

When I see the orphans standing on the cold sidewalk, I hope there will never again be such a war.

琴焚きて雪夜を寝ねず引揚げし
かの日思へばなに耐へざらむ

大阪　香島八重子

Returning to our homeland. In the cold sleepless winter night, we burned our Koto. When I think about those hard days, I realize I can overcome anything. (Koto: Japanese harp)

ふたたびはくりかへさじと悔深く軍事法廷の記事を読みつぐ

三重　宇城直一

As I continue to read the article about the military tribunal, my determination grows. This must never happen again.

広島の焼野にたちし棟長屋
ゆふべ点く灯のあたたかく見ゆ

広島　加藤賚作

The temporary housing set up in the burnt fields of Hiroshima, I see the lanterns, I can feel warmth in them all.

焼(や)けはてし街(まち)にかへりて大工(だいく)われ
まごころこめて握(にぎ)るのみかも

静岡　淺野高夫

Returning to my burnt and desolate hometown. I, the carpenter, put my heart and soul into holding my chisel.

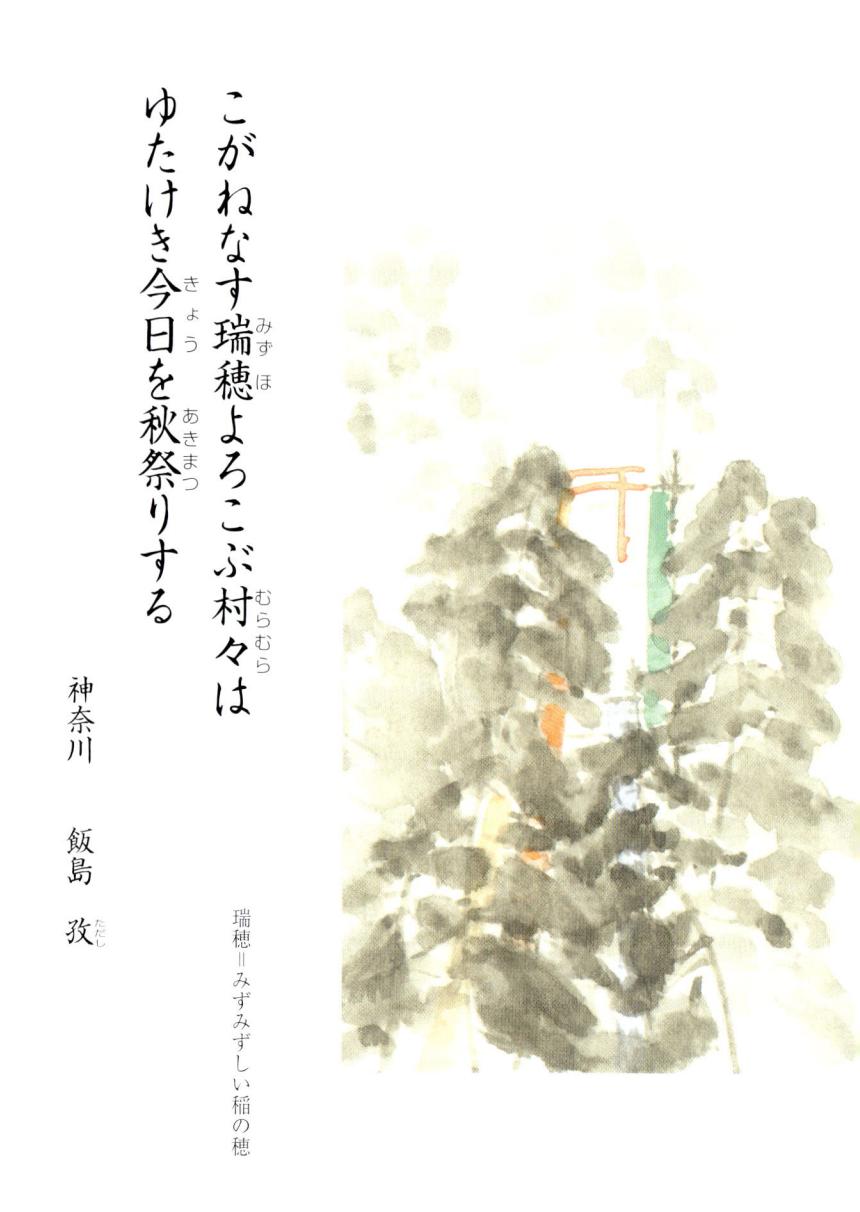

こがねなす瑞穂(みずほ)よろこぶ村々(むらむら)は
ゆたけき今日(きょう)を秋祭(あきまつ)りする

神奈川　飯島　孜(ただし)

瑞穂＝みずみずしい稲の穂

The rice fields are golden, a good harvest has come. The villagers take delight in holding an autumn festival.

山（やま）ふかくきこりの業（わざ）をはげみつつ
世（よ）びとの幸（さち）を祈（いの）りてやまず

東京　田中粒志

Deep in the mountains, I strive as a woodcutter. I pray for people's happiness.

山に住めば山は親しも炭やきを
よすぎとしつつ悔ゆることなし

宮城　佐藤一郎

世過ぎ＝生活

I enjoy working as a charcoal burner living in the mountains. I have no regrets choosing this way of living.

土の香の身にしみつきてつつがなく
子らうちそろひ畑うつはたのし

静岡　立石正太郎

The smell of the soil surrounding me, it's wonderful to plough the fields with my children.

小女等が繊手にはげむ眞心は
糸にこもりて平和結ばむ

岡山　進藤蒼太郎

繊手＝かぼそい手

The young girls spinning with their fine slender fingers. Their devotion pours into the fine threads. It will bring peace.

雪捨つる海の青さのいやまさる
港はるかに捕鯨船ゆく

群馬　大熊常雄

The sea in which we dispose of excess snow, a blue deeper than blue. I can see the whaling ship leaving.

刈(かり)入(い)れも事(こと)なく終(お)へて爐(ろ)を囲(かこ)む
秋(あき)の長夜(よなが)は楽(たの)しかりけり

滋賀　廣瀬徹夫

The harvest finished smoothly. Now we really love the long autumn nights in front of the fireplace.

今宵(こよい)また暮(く)れゆく海(うみ)をゆく船(ふね)に
さきはひあれと灯(ひ)ともすわれは

富山　高柳芳雄

I see a ship sailing in the evening. I wish it peace and happiness as I, the lighthouse keeper, continue to light its path.

みどりよりみどりに暮るるわが家は
草ぶきなれど心やすけし

神奈川　宮地佑閣

The sun settles on my hut surrounded by nature greener than green. It is a humble thatched hut, but staying here provides me with peace.

山住みの夏こそよけれ子とひたる
野風呂あまねき月夜となりぬ

神奈川　和久井小史

Enjoying an outdoor bath with my children in the moonlight makes me think, living in the mountains in summer is wonderful.

野(の)に遊(あそ)ぶ子(こ)が吹(ふ)きならす麦笛(むぎぶえ)の
さやかなる音(ね)の響(ひび)く頃(ころ)かも

愛媛　朝井恭堂

The children are playing in the field. The bright sound of them blowing their pipes made from wheat is echoing around.

昇(のぼ)る日(ひ)のひかり仰(あお)ぎてわれ願(ねが)ふ
国々(くにぐに)の幸(さち)人々(ひとびと)の幸(さち)

滋賀　竹村たか子

Looking up at the rising sun, my wish is for all countries and people to be happy.

人類(じんるい)がたたかひの爐(ろ)に投(な)げ入(い)れし
さちの価(あたい)はいくばくならむ

東京　關根京平

What is the value of our happiness that we threw into the fire for the sake of war?

明(あ)け暮(く)れを清水(しみず)乏(とも)しく湧(わ)く島(しま)に
おごらぬ人(ひと)ら住(す)みていそしむ

宮城　島田白虹

On the island with springs of pure water, people who have been humbled live and work diligently.

山河は幼き夢のままにして
吾が故郷の稔り豊けき

山形　松井　幸

The mountains and rivers are the same as in my childhood dreams, now our crops are abundant.

手鞠唄(てまりうた)のどかに子等(こら)の遊(あそ)びゐて
平和(へいわ)の春(はる)はありがたきかも

福岡　花田静枝

As I witness the song of the children playing with a ball, I give thanks for this spring in peace.

ふるさとにかへり来りて光降る
大空の下青き麦踏む

秋田　木澤長太郎

Back in the fields of my hometown, I tread on the new shoots of wheat in the sunshine under this grand sky.

坑口を出でし明るさのびのびと
朝空仰ぎ腕を伸ばしぬ

群馬　鶴田　稔

I come out of the mine, I feel relaxed as I extend my arms and look up to the brightness of the morning sky.

馬曳きて野辺に出づれば百鳥の
こゑも平和を讃ふるごとし

東京　福村長青

I bring my horse to the field. Hundreds of birds are singing as if they are proclaiming peace.

雪原は早春のひかりにかがやきて
見わたす限り動くものなし

秋田　富士村春宵

The snow covered fields are shining in the early spring sunlight. As far as I can see, nothing moves.

そばの花咲ける畠の露じめり
蟲鳴く宵は母の恋ひしき

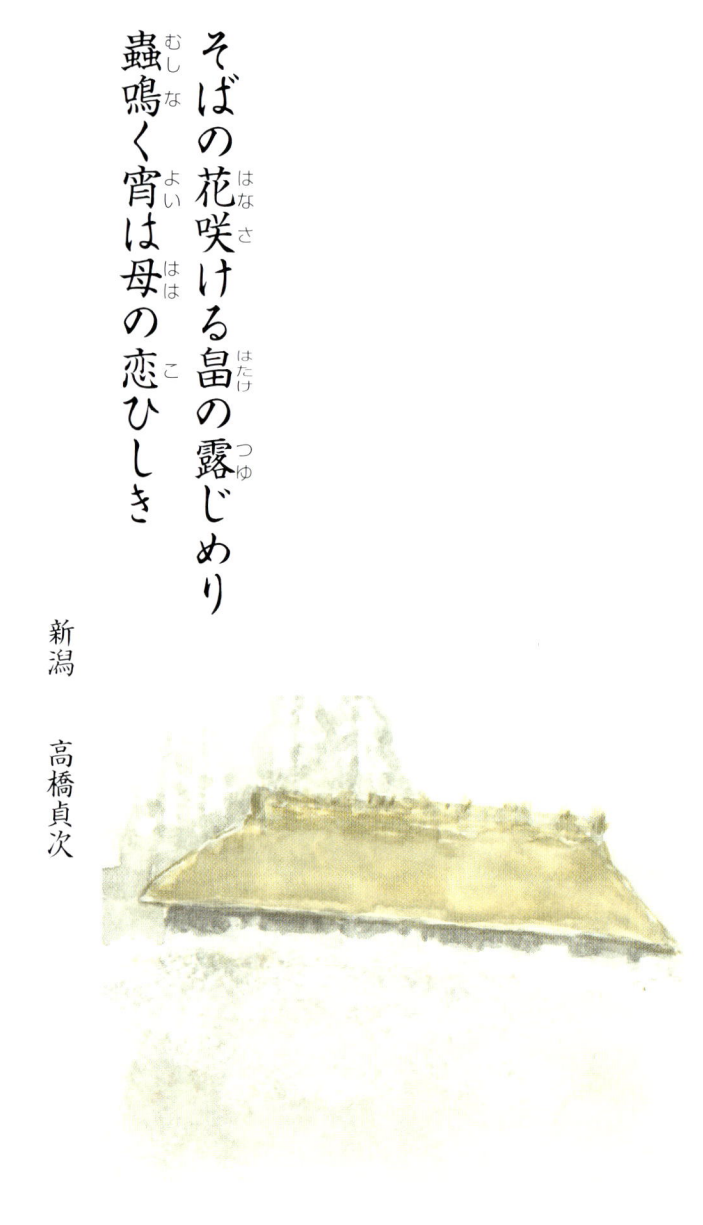

新潟　高橋貞次

The flowering fields of Soba are covered with dew. As I listen to the chirping insects in the evening, I really miss my mother.

力限り働くはたのし朝風に
曳き出づる馬はいななきにけり

埼玉　保永不沙夫

I like working with all my might. In the morning wind, my horse lets out a strong whine.

再建のみ国に生きておのが田を
守りつつ悔なき一生終へなむ

宮城　坂本秀治

We are embarking on the rebuilding of our country. I hope to cultivate my own land and live my life without regret until the end.

平和の鐘響かふ聞けば心澄み
わが生ける幸今日も湧き来る

東京　橘　馨

When I hear the sweet reverberations of the bell of peace, everything becomes clear with the happiness that I am living today flowing into me.

もやごもり明け来る峡の木ぬれより
光りて見ゆる浦の朝凪

京都　尾城成節

I can see the calm morning sea shining at me through a gap in the trees of the foggy valley at dawn.

朝露（あさつゆ）に紅緒（べにお）ぬらしてもぐ茄子（なす）の
かごに溢（あふ）るるわが家（いえ）の幸（さち）

東京　斉藤禮子

The straps of my sandals got wet from the morning dew while picking eggplants.
My basket full of fresh eggplants, my family's happiness.

よみがへる我(わ)が日(ひ)の本(もと)の春(はる)たけて
小(お)川(がわ)の岸(きし)に土筆(つくし)つむ子(こ)等(ら)

埼玉　本橋紫良

The mid spring of our recovering country. Children are picking Tsukushi shoots on the stream bank.

眞清水の湧きてやまざるその如く
わが世も人も清くあらまし

青森　池野永奇

Just like the never-ending pure water bubbling from the well, I hope we all can live like that.

兵(へい)となる事(こと)しあらねばすこやけく
吾子(あこ)育(そだ)てつつ安(やす)けし母(はは)は

神奈川　黒澤　綠

My mother can now happily raise her children, safe in the thought that her son won't be drafted into the army.

さきがけて和を尊むとのたまひし
聖徳太子ありがたきかな

東京　井浦敦子

As the well respected Shotoku-Taishi said, harmony should come before everything.

製材の鋸音絶えしひとときを
麦の穂波の輝きて見ゆ

広島　福本逸男

As the whirling sound of the wood saw dies down, I see the ears of wheat shining in the field.

雲がくり月ほのかなる雨の夜を
傘さしゆけば花みかん匂ふ

和歌山　鹽崎　曠

In the rainy evening, a dim light comes from the moon slightly hiding behind the clouds. I put up my umbrella as the sweet fragrance of the citrus blossoms hangs in the air.

内海の島のいくつも行くふねも
みむらさきに匂ふしづけさ

香川　梶　カツエ

The ships are coming and going between the islands of the inland sea. Their silent journey creates a pale violet haze.

夜(よ)も昼(ひる)も心(こころ)やすけし人(ひと)のいのち
尊(たふと)まるる世(よ)になりしと思(おも)へば

埼玉　麻生恭二

I have peace of mind day and night now that we have come to a time where there is respect for human life.

ひたすらに種(たね)播(ま)く人(ひと)の姿(すがた)よし
ゆらぐがごとき光(ひかり)のなかに

東京　山本勇市

The majestic figure of a man, focused on the task of sowing seeds. It seems to flicker in the evaporating haze.

たえまなく若狭(わかさ)の湾(わん)をいさり船(ぶね)
大漁(たいりょう)の幟(のぼり)たてて入(い)りくる

福井　武永　榮

いさり船＝魚を捕る舟

In Wakasa bay, the fishing boats are coming and going without pause. The ones with a large catch raise their flags to mark the event.

やすき世(よ)に生(い)きて働(はたら)くよろこびに
みなみち足(た)りて思(おも)ふことなし

大阪　中山勝代

Living and working in peace. Nobody could want more than this.

かがやける光を見れば草も木も
人の子もみなめぐまれてあり

滋賀　井上肇國

When I see the sparkling sun light, I wish the grass, the trees and the people to be blessed.

鳥の声澄み透りゆく朝みどり
静かに天つ光満ち来ぬ

群馬　一場譽志雄

It's morning, the sound of the birds chirping permeates through the green leaves. The day is quietly being filled with sunlight.

乏(とも)しかる乳(ちち)に生(お)ひゆくみどり児(ご)も
次(つぎ)の代(よ)背負(せお)ふ一人(ひとり)なるかも

東京　成宮芳三郎

ともし＝とぼしい

Our babies living with barely enough milk will some day take the reigns and become citizens supporting our country.

新(あたら)しき日(ひ)を迎(むか)へたりいまさらに
世(せ)界(かい)につづく海(うみ)のひろさよ

茨城　小神野藤花

We are at the dawn of a new time. I feel the vastness of the sea which connects the whole world.

いささかの善(よ)きことありて始(はじ)まりし
日(ひ)はひねもすを楽(たの)しかりけり

東京　前田良治

ひねもす＝朝から夕まで

When the day starts with a little bit of good luck, I am happy for the rest of the day.

あらがねの土を拓きて萌え出づる
いのちはぐくみ花咲かせなむ

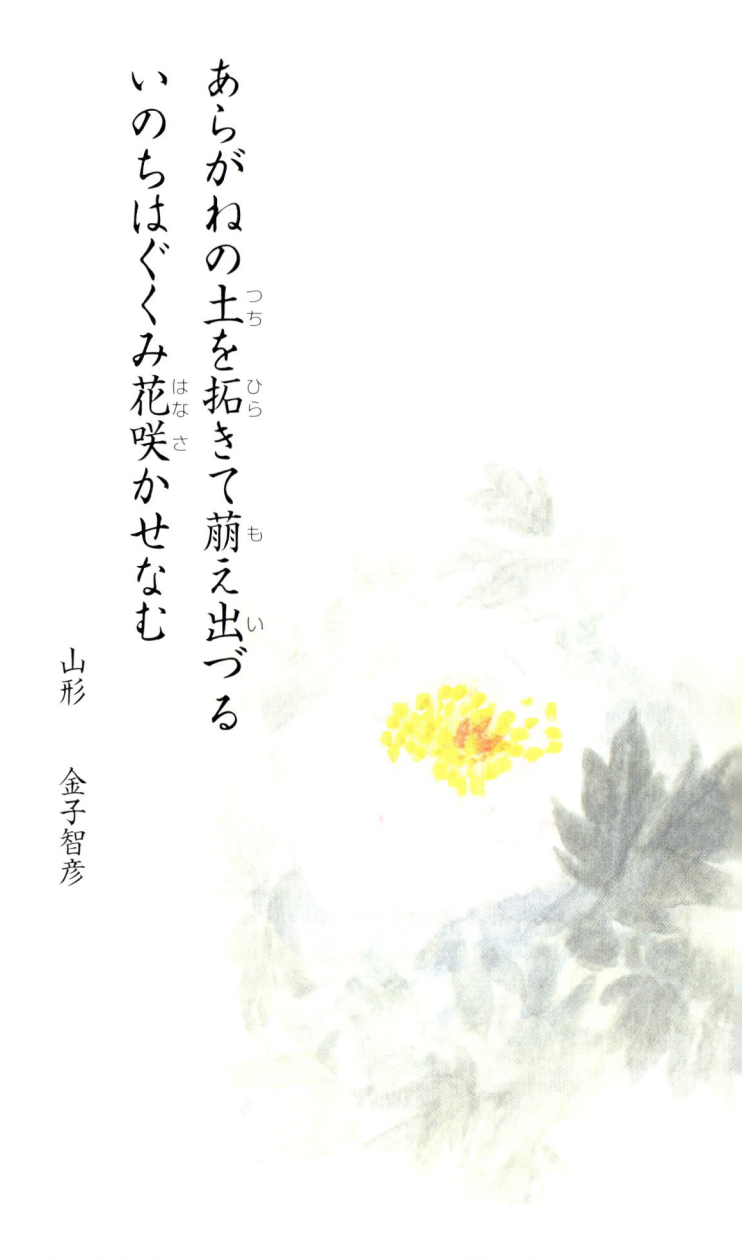

山形　金子智彦

Opening up the rough earth, a little shoot sprouts out. It will nurture life and bloom a beautiful flower.

億兆の祈りをこめて萬代に
平和の鐘を鳴り響かさむ

東京　大貫正義

With the prayers of millions, we will ring the bell of peace and let it echo all around the world.

ただ祈る世界の人のおほらけく
こころひとつにむすばるる日を

東京　近藤英治

All I pray for is the welfare of all the people in the world. May all our hearts be united as one.

遠国(とおぐに)の誰(た)が装(よそ)ふべき衣(きぬ)ならむ
筬(おさ)持つ日々(ひび)をさくら散(ち)りつぐ

香川　河西さよ子

筬＝織機の付属具

I sit here weaving cloth. Outside, cherry blossom petals are fluttering down. I wonder who will wear these clothes in a far away land.

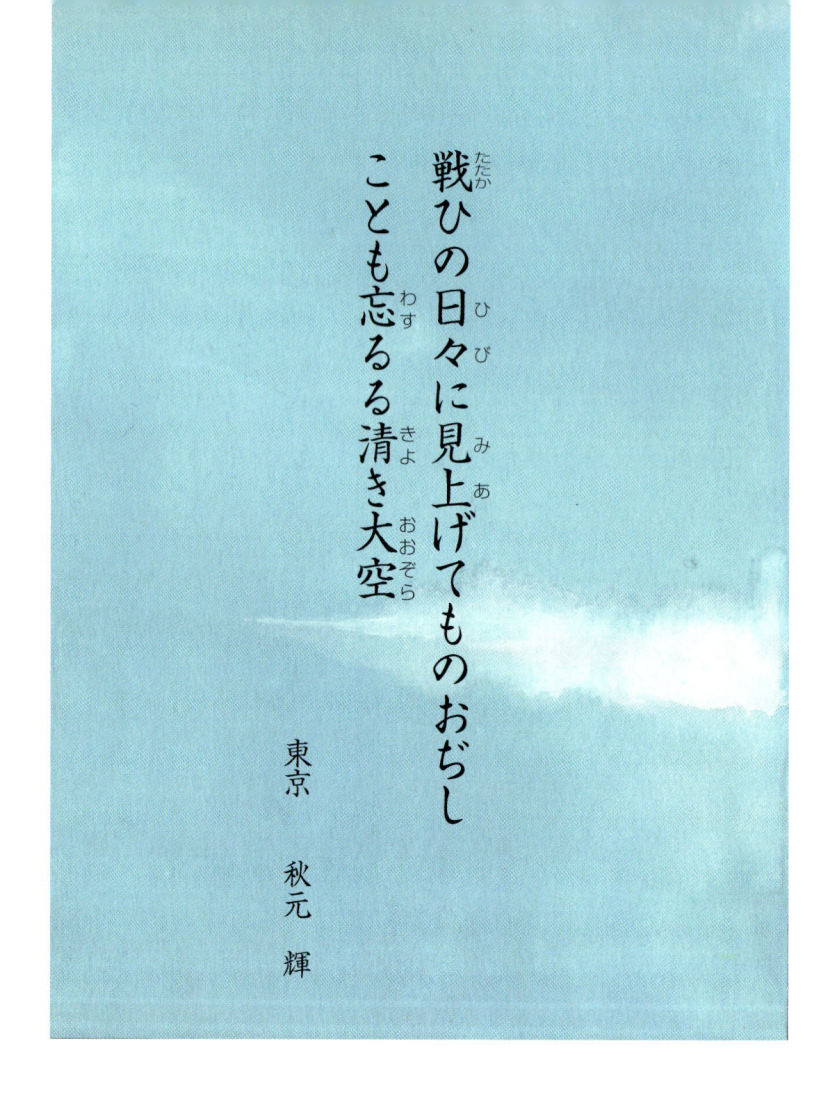

戦(たたか)ひの日々(ひび)に見上(みあ)げてものおぢし
こども忘(わす)るる清(きよ)き大空(おおぞら)

東京　秋元　輝

The clear blue sky above me. I can now forget the feeling of times of war, looking up to the sky in fear.

天地(あめつち)のはてまでひびけ日(ひ)の本(もと)の
平和(へいわ)の鐘(かね)は今(いま)鳴(な)り渡(わた)る

東京　志萱正男

The bell of peace is ringing. Echoing loudly to all ends of the earth.

糸垂れてわれうつつなし天地に
ただひとつなる浮標守りつつ

茨城　大鳥井金一郎

I cast my fishing line and my mind is clear. I focus all my attention on the float.

入（い）っ日（ひ）に想（おも）ひは深（ふか）し悔（く）ゆるなく
君（きみ）にとつがむ日（ひ）は迫（せま）りつつ

大阪　田古里文子

On the eve of my wedding, in deep thought, I have no regrets. Soon I will be married.

人の世もみな美しく思ほえて
降らむばかりの星仰ぎゐつ

栃木　新勝

Looking up to the star strewn night sky makes me think, everything in this world is beautiful.

さくら散る牧場の流れ浅ければ
仔馬らよりて水を飲みをり

愛知　大塚邦夫

By the shallow stream on the farm where the cherry blossom petals have fallen, the ponies gather to drink.

はるやまにももちの花の匂ふごと
笑み交はしつつ世を送らばや

和歌山　水谷久吉

I long to live my life, exchanging smiles as beautiful as the sweet fragrance of thousands of flowers in the spring mountains.

いやつぎて湧きくる朝の雲白く
光らむとして秋の富士澄む

静岡　窪井朝陽

The majestic Mt. Fuji sits clearly in the shining light of the morning. Clouds of pure white are flowing out.

さくさくと草刈る音も遠のきつ
朝もや分けて陽はさしのぼる

新潟　坂田なほ

The sound of grass cutting fades away, as the sun breaks through the morning mist.

朝露を葉の面にとどめはつはつに
白蓮の花ひらき初めたり

東京　桐　俊子

はつはつ＝かすかにあらわれるさま

Leaves coated with droplets of pure morning dew. The white lotus blossoms.

おほらかに蒼穹(そら)の地球(ちきゅう)を包(つつ)むごと
人(ひと)も垣(かき)せずむつみゆかまし

東京　市村　宏

Like the atmosphere that softly coats this earth, people should live together, overcoming all barriers.

田作りの吾ならねども健やけく
伸びたる稲田見ればうれしも

東京　田中敏太郎

Although I am unable to help with the farm work, I am filled with a sense of joy from watching the rice flourish in the paddies.

月光を慕ひて来にし松林
幹の片側白くあかるし

神奈川　衞藤豊治

My longing for the moonlight drew me to the pine forest. One side of the tree trunk is lit up bright white.

たなそこをあゆむ蛍のやはらかき
光は妻の顔に映えつつ

たなそこ＝てのひら

山形　雨宮蕾圃

The fireflies are softly glowing in my wife's hands. Their light reflects upon her face.

山桜日のあるかぎりかがよひて
夜は月光に濡れてひそけし

東京　新井更二

The wild cherry blossoms are radiant during the day. At night, they are calm and moist.

たちさわぐ浪(なみ)をさまりてわたの原(はら)
こぎゆく船(ふね)の船唄(ふなうた)のどか

北海道　田中政一

The wild waves of the storm have calmed down. As he rows out to sea, the sailor's song echoes peacefully.

百のうた　千の想い

大竹桂子

新春の講義

「私の家には、祖母・星野せいが残した大切なカルタがあります。祖母は、大変美しい人だと私は子ども心にも思ったものでした。今日はそのカルタにまつわるお話をしたいと思います」

一月七日、夫が「新春に百人一首を味わう」というタイトルで話をした。場所は吉祥寺村立雑学大学。大学は授業料、参加料、会場料の三つがタダ、全てボランティアで運営されていて、二十八年目を迎える。私たちはこの大学のメンバーで毎週授業に出席し、時に講師も務めている。この日、私は和服で薄茶のおもてなしをした。

このとき、画家の稲田善樹さんを誘った。彼とは今までに二冊の絵本を創る仕事をしている。満州からの引揚者である彼は、平和を祈る気持ちがことに強い人である。かねてから祖母のカルタに興味を抱いていた。カルタのうたは、終戦直後に募集された平和百人一首である。そこに応募した祖母は、

　外つ国の人も愛づらむ咲き足りて
　日傘に舞ひ散る桜吹雪は

この一首が入選した。一男四女の子どもたちに、筆書きのカルタを残している。その数は取り札と、読み札で二百枚、子ども五人で千枚にもおよぶものである。戦後の物が不足している時代、紙の調達には苦心したようだ。取り札には写真の台帳が使われたり、固い紙で裏打ちをしたものもある。きちんと裁断された紙に、流れるような美しい筆文字、それは行書や草書体が使われ、判読はかなり難しいものである。

星野せいは、明治十八年九月三日に信州中込の造り酒屋の娘として生まれた。その後、岩村田の繭問屋・星野虎雄と結婚した。晩年は東京世田谷二子玉川で暮らし、昭和三十七年七十八歳で亡くなっている。私たちがお正月に母の家を訪ねると、夜みんなでこのカルタをとり終えるまでは、家には帰れなかったものだ。息子と娘が幼いとき、カルタのひと文字が読めるくらいの年齢からとっていた。この習慣は夫にも受け継がれ、孫が高校生になった今も続いている。

講義の終わり、カルタになった百首の短歌に、絵を添えて本に纏めてみたい、と夫は宣言した。

カルタから書き写す

夫との二人三脚でカルタのうたを書き写す作業が始まる。筆文字は、ときどきおや？と思われる字もある。そんなときは『五體字類』で調べる。辞書には字の略し方が載っており、どういう字からできているのか一字ずつ確かめていく。苦しんだのは、草書で描かれた名前の判読であった。一本の線が何からできてい

資料調べ

二月のある日、永田町にある国立国会図書館に出向いた。入館のとき驚いたのは、コートやバックなど私物を館内に持ち込めないことだった。これらはロッカーに収め、必要な物は透明な袋に入れ、名前を登録して入る。本の検索はパソコンの操作をしなければならない。慣れないので係りの助けを借りて、探していた一冊の本を手にした。

平和の鐘楼建立委員会編『平和百人一首 和英対訳』、昭和二十五年に編纂されたものである。傷みやすいのでコピーはできない、と注意書きがある。薄い小さなサイズで片手にのる本を手にしたとき、感動を覚えた。大切に大切に作られていたからだ。

表紙には鳥の子和紙が使われ、見出しに四枚のカラーで四季の絵が添えられていた。絵は安田靫彦、小林古径など一流の画家、絵にはパラフィン紙がかけられている。ページをめくると、永井隆、湯川秀樹などの有名人や歌人の歌集で、募集された短歌ではない。夕暮れまで図書館にいたが、何の手がかりも見つけられなかった。

各新聞社に聞き合わせても「平和百人一首」の検索では、膨大なものがあるという。自分で出向き、戦後

の新聞縮小版を調べてみたが、募集記事を見つけられない。何も分からないまま、どうすればいいのだろうかと途方にくれた。

そんなときである。稲田さんからうれしい情報が飛び込んできた。

大学で司書の仕事をしている高橋隆一郎さんが、国立国会図書館に出向き、調査してくれたという。高橋さんの綿密な調べから多くの資料が出てきた。闇の世界に沈んでいたうたが、六十年近い歳月を経て、すーっと薄明かりの中に浮上した。

平和百人一首の募集記事は、読売新聞・昭和二十三年四月八日付け朝刊二面で見つけた。募集主は、平和の鐘楼建立会、入賞者には一首二百円とある。これは新憲法記念事業の一つとして行われている。資料補修のために閲覧できない雑誌に載っているという記事を調べに再び国立国会図書館に行く。検閲のかかったゲラはアメリカのメリーランド大学図書館に「プランゲ文庫」として集められているという。そのマイクロフィッシュ雑誌が、憲政資料室にあった。

シート状のフィルムに焼き付けられたものを、一枚ずつ調べ、十八首の短歌を見つける。それは昭和二十三年発行『文章倶楽部』「短歌と生活する」（鈴木實著）にあった。掲載された短歌は、二万三千七百二十の応募者の中から予選を通過したものであった。ここに残った百五十首からさらに選が進められている。

長い間、祖母のカルタで親しんできたうたが、印刷文字で現われたとき、いっそう親しみを覚えた。

子どもたちに、世界の人たちに

私は「むさしのスカーレットアジアお話の会」で子どもたちにアジアの本を読み聞かせる活動をしている。

平和百人一首を本にしたいと仲間に話した。すると、野崎斐子さんが英訳を添えたいという、

「アジアや欧米の人々は、日本をよく知らないと思うのよ。外国から日本は批判されているけど、戦争が終わったとき、庶民がどんな気持ちをもって暮らしていたか、ぜひ、海外の人たちにも分かってほしいの」

彼女は英語が堪能。アジアの絵本を訳す仕事をしている。強い助っ人が現われ、輪がひろがってきた。

画家の稲田さんからメールが入っている。

「今、一冊の絵本を仕上げています。その仕事を終えたら、八月からカルタの絵を描きます」と。

うたには長い戦から解き放たれ、ささやかな喜びにひたる庶民の姿がある。その内容はやさしさに満ち溢れている。故郷の自然や働く喜び、家族や平和な日本をいとおしむ気持ちが滲んでいる。分かりやすい言葉で綴られたうたに感動した彼は、二十枚の絵を依頼したのに、百枚全部描くという。その情熱を凄いと思いながら、百枚のカラーページの本と考えただけで、挫折しそう。多額の出版資金はどこから捻出すればいいのだろう……。

ときに、売れないかもしれない「平和百人一首」の本を、なぜ、私がつくるのか、そう自問自答を繰り返すのだった。そんなときは、ゆったりと墨をすり、柔らかな和紙に筆でうたを書いてみる。

　春の野をわが恋ひくればみなし児の
　くろき片手にれんげ匂へり

琴焚きて雪夜を寝ねず引揚げし
かの日思へばなに耐へざらむ

魂のごちそう

慎ましやかな調べに、萎えた心が癒され、勇気づけられる。選ばれた百首は、百人のうたではある。けれども、戦後の混乱の中で二万数千人の応募があったことを考えると、かぎりなく多くの人たちの思いが、この百首に凝縮されていると思う。うたには純粋で美しい日本の心が、一つの大河のように流れている。

現代は物がありながら、心が荒んでいるかにみえる。だからこそ今、この魂の歓びのうたを味わい、感じて欲しい。

「平和百人一首」が募集されてから六十年目のこの春、うたを甦らせたい、深い祈りをこめて編みました。

これは会誌『KEG』（平成十九年度木村治美エッセイストクラブ）十八号に掲載したものに手を加えたものです。

結びのことば

「平和百人一首」にこめられた庶民の祈りや喜びは、このままでは歴史の大きな流れの中で、消えてしまうかも知れない、そんな思いがあります。祖母せいの手造りカルタにこめられた大切な美しい日本の心を、次の世代に伝えなければいけない、そう考えて本に纏めました。

作者のお名前は、東洋大学図書館、国際日本文化研究センター図書館の貴重な資料で確認させていただきました。短歌が募集されてから、あまりに長い歳月が経ち、一人ひとりのご承諾をいただく術はありませんでした。版権をお持ちの方も、どうぞ寛大なお心でご容赦くださいますよう、お願い申しあげます。

英訳の野崎斐子さん、トーマス・ロウさんは、ボランティアでご協力をいただきました。温もりのある挿絵の稲田善樹さん、みんな、でき得る限りの力を結集し、平和への祈りをこめ、この本をつくりあげました。またお力を本を編むにあたって、北海道室蘭市に在住の小笠原洽嘉先生から沢山のご指導を賜りました。いただいた皆さまには、心からの感謝を申しあげます。

平成二十年二月二日

編者　大竹桂子
監修　大竹隆一
平和を祈る画家　稲田善樹
対訳者　Thomas Low
　　　　野崎斐子

大竹桂子（おおたけ　けいこ）
1937年、高知県生まれ。東京都武蔵野市在住。木村治美エッセイストグループ会員。モンゴルの子どもたちに絵本を贈る「むさしのビーンズクラブ」代表。アジアを考え行動する「むさしのスカーレット・アジアお話の会」で仲間と一緒にアジアの本を訳し、子どもたちに読み聞かせする活動を行っている。ジャンビーン・ダシドントク作モンゴル創作民話『みどりの馬』（てらいんく）翻訳。

稲田善樹（いなだ　よしき）
1939年、中国・旧満州生まれ。
1979年以来アジア諸国他取材、平和をテーマに個展開催
絵本制作もてがける。

英訳協力	表紙織布
武蔵野市国際交流協会	染織り処岩清
会員　野崎斐子	岩田重信・金由起
会員　Thomas Low	新潟県十日町市中条

百のうた　千の想い
——甦る平和百人一首——

発行日　二〇〇八年五月三日　初版第一刷発行

編者　大竹桂子
装挿画　稲田善樹
発行者　佐相美佐枝
発行所　株式会社てらいんく
〒二一五-〇〇〇七　川崎市麻生区向原三-一四-七
TEL　〇四四-九五三-一八二八
FAX　〇四四-九五九-一八〇三
振替　〇〇一五〇-八五四七一

印刷所　厚徳社

© 2008 Printed in Japan
© Keiko Otake & Yoshiki Inada　ISBN978-4-86261-025-6 C0095

落丁・乱丁のお取り替えは送料小社負担でいたします。
直接小社制作部までお送りください。

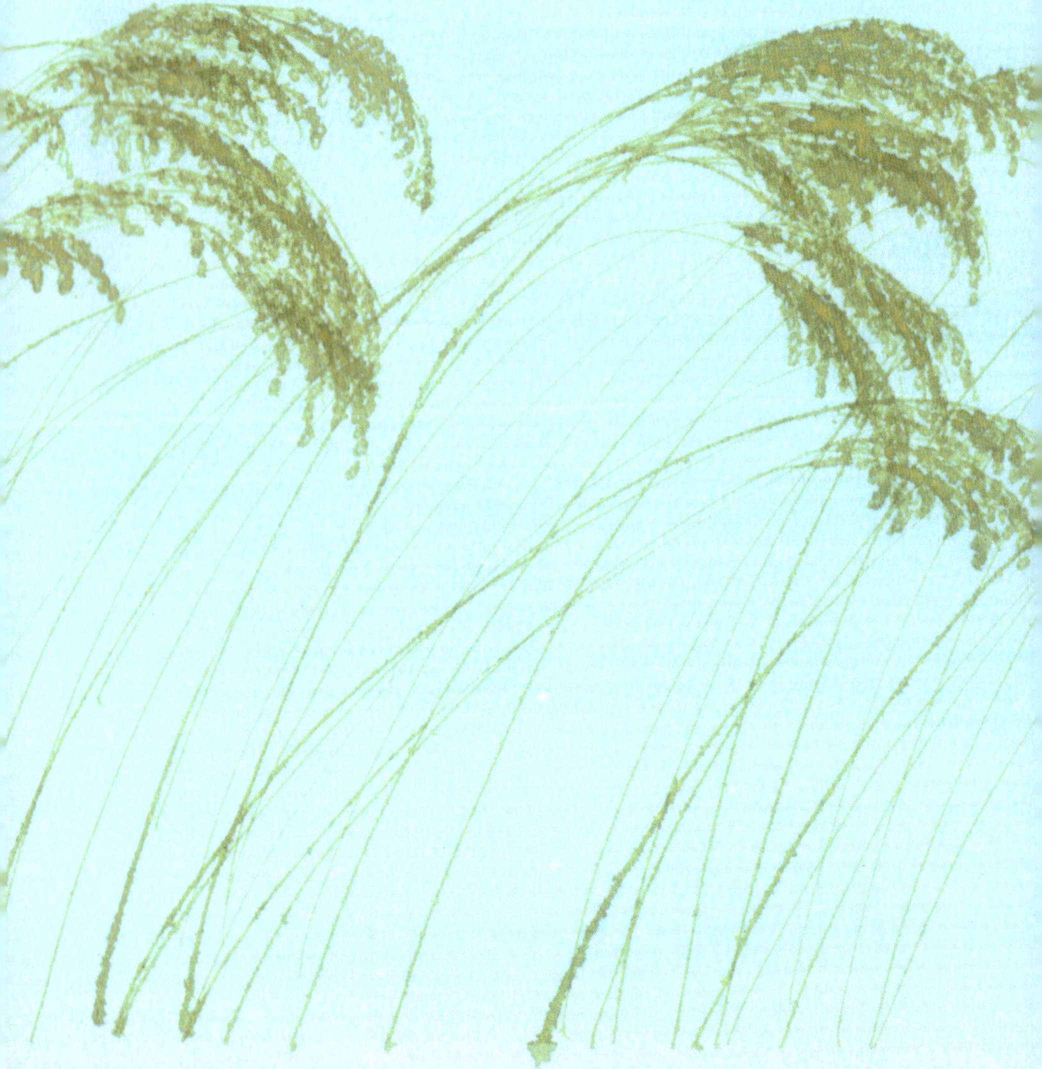